My Dog

Written by June Crebbin

Illustrated by Russell Ayto

WALKER BOOKS
AND SUBSIDIARIES

LONDON · BOSTON · SYDNEY

My dog is ...

a loud-barker

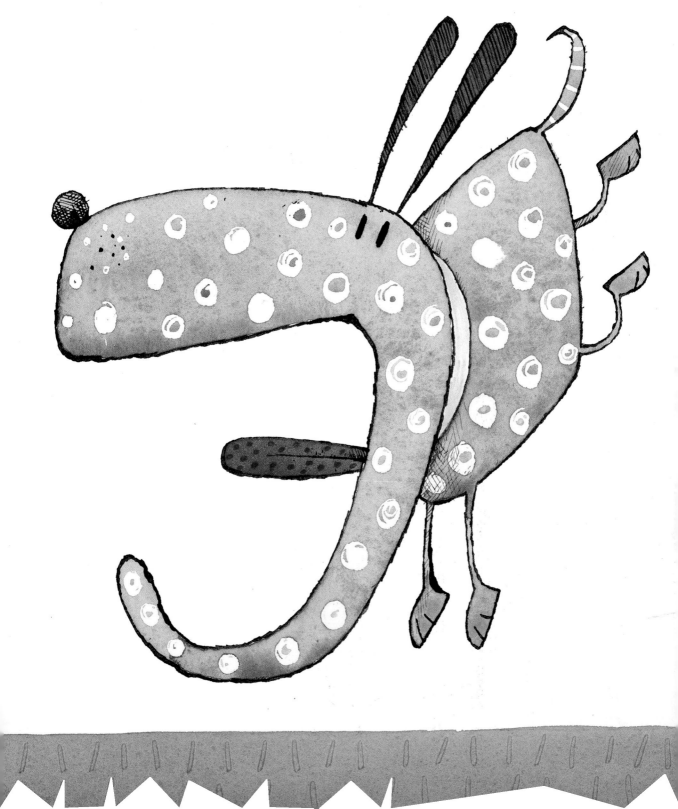

a fast-runner

a food-gobbler

a stick-fetcher

a hole-digger

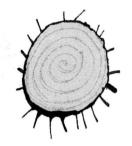

a sun-snoozer

a cat-chaser

a body-warmer

a tail-wagger

and ...

MY BEST FRIEND!

For Will
J.C.
For Greta
R.A.

First published 2001 by Walker Books Ltd
87 Vauxhall Walk, London SE11 5HJ

2 4 6 8 10 9 7 5 3 1

Text © 2001 June Crebbin
Illustrations © 2001 Russell Ayto

This book has been typeset in Avant Garde

Printed in Hong Kong

British Library Cataloguing in Publication Data:
a catalogue record for this book is available
from the British Library

ISBN 0-7445-8308-X